This Orchard
book belongs to

....

....

....

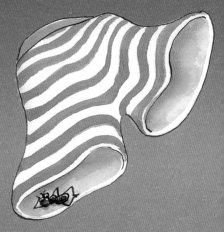

To Andrea, who keeps
me on my toes – J.J.

For little Rosie – G.P-R.

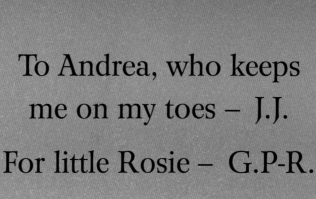

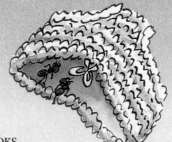
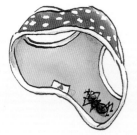

ORCHARD BOOKS
338 Euston Road, London NW1 3BH
Orchard Books Australia
Level 17/207 Kent Street, Sydney, NSW 2000

First published in 2010 by Orchard Books
First paperback publication in 2011

ISBN 978 1 40830 525 6

Text © Julia Jarman 2010
Illustrations © Guy Parker-Rees 2010

A CIP catalogue record for this book is available
from the British Library.

3 5 7 9 10 8 6 4

Printed in China

Orchard Books is a division of Hachette Children's Books,
an Hachette UK company.

www.hachette.co.uk

Julia Jarman 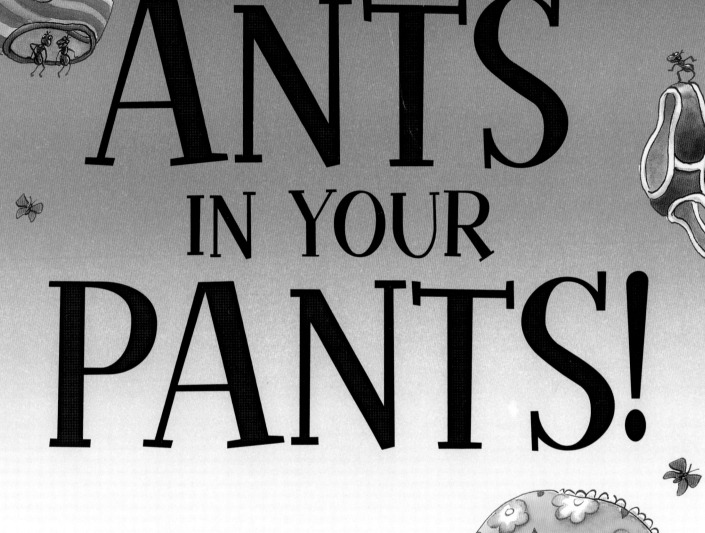 Guy Parker-Rees

ANTS
IN YOUR
PANTS!

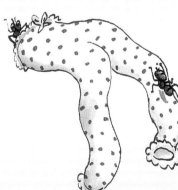

ORCHARD

Leopard was having a party.

"But only
for really
cool dudes.

Please, DO NOT tell Aardvark.
He doesn't like party food."

Leopard got ever so anxious
About the food and the drink.

"What about my
birthday cake?

Blue candles,
    don't you think?"

"But don't, do NOT, tell Aardvark.
He really mustn't know.
He only eats ants and cucumbers . . .

And he slurps
them down
in one go!"

Now Aardvark wasn't that bothered
(And he *did* hear the word going round),

But he liked to roam . . .

or play at home . . .

With Big Sis under the ground.

But *someone* was *very* offended
Not to get one of
Leopard's invites.

Big Ant hurried home
and got on the phone, "There's a party
at Leopard's tonight."

Now ants really like parties.
They enjoy a good bop with their chums.

They like party food

and games that are rude –

Like *Who Can Bite
the Most Bums?*

The party guests started arriving,
Unaware of Big Ant's secret plot:

"First get to Leopard's party, then find yourself a bot."

The guests didn't hear the order
To all the other cross ants . . .

"Wait until everyone's eating,

Then start playing *ANTS IN YOUR PANTS!*"

"Let's party!" Leopard said loudly,
And everyone started to sing.

Nobody saw
the chomping jaws
Of ants getting ready to sting!

Then Croc cried, "Can we start eating?
I want some lollies on sticks!"

"Me too! Me too!"
cried Cockatoo.

Big Ant said,

"START BITING! BE QUICK!"

Suddenly Leopard was leaping
Ever so high in the air,

Tearing off
his best trousers

And showing
his underwear!

Soon all the guests were jumping,
Throwing their pants in the air,

Trying to stop
   those naughty ants –

Some of their
   bottoms were
   bare!

Meanwhile . . .

   Aardvark and Big Sis felt hungry,
Ants *were* their favourite food,

So they set off to
   sniff out some supper,
But stopped –

            when they saw something rude . . .

The sky was full of knickers!
There were party pants
everywhere!

BIG ONES,

small ones,

FRILLY ONES,

TALL ONES,

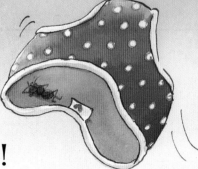

Whizzing through the air!

"What *is* going on?" asked Big Sis,
Watching Elephant hop.

"Oh, it's the party," said Aardvark.
"They're having
a bit of a bop."

"We didn't get an invite,
But while we're here let's feast."

He stuck out his tongue,

"Yummy,
yum,
yum!"

"Cor! Thanks!"
sighed Wilderbeest.

"Why *didn't* you invite us?"
Said Aardvark, wrinkling his snout.
"I'm really sorry," said Leopard.
"I was wrong to leave you out."

"I'll tell you something though,"
he smiled,
As Big Sis licked his ear.

"Now, you'll *both* be invited
To my party every year!"